Daughters of the Vicar

Daughters of the Vicar

D.H. Lawrence

ET REMOTISSIMA PROPE

Hesperus Classics

Hesperus Classics
Published by Hesperus Press Limited
4 Rickett Street, London sw6 1ru
www.hesperuspress.com

First published in *The Prussian Officer and Other Stories* in 1914
First published by Hesperus Press Limited, 2004

Foreword © Anita Desai, 2004

Designed and typeset by Fraser Muggeridge
Printed in Italy by Graphic Studio Srl

isbn: 1-84391-0-837

CONTENTS

FOREWORD

If Lawrence had not left England in search of sun and health, if he had not travelled to Mexico and Italy and Australia, his oeuvre would have been a very different one. In *Daughters of the Vicar*, a short story he wrote in 1911, one can find all the themes, subjects, motifs and images that would have formed his entire territory if he had not left the damp, mossy soil in which they are rooted for dramatically different ones.

What grew out of it was Lawrence's troubled and painful view of life and society, darkened by the shadows cast by coal hills, smokestacks and stone walls. He saw life as essentially a struggle of opposites and it is in that tension that his stories hang as from a web of highly strung and dangerous electric wires.

At the most basic level – one that Lawrence took very seriously – there are the different physical types: the strong, healthy and attractive one ('ruddy with the sun… his figure, a straight, fine jet of life') and the puny, sickly, weak one ('What a little abortion!'); as well as the opposites of the colour spectrum, fair and dark ('the nape of her neck was very white, with fine down and pointed wisps of gold' and 'His black face and arms were uncouth, he was foreign. His face was masked black with coal-dust… What was he, as he sat there in his pit dirt?'). The different types of character create a natural opposition too – the type that is led by cool, clear rationalism and the type that is ruled by a warm and turbulent heart; the type that imposes its will, coldly and even cruelly, as if to test it, and the type that submits to it, out of weakness, inertia or attraction.

Lawrence was more than an observer of human beings in the way of a novelist, however. He was a thinker with his theories, a philosopher and a proselytiser, interested in the bitter and complicated opposites created by a society based on economics. He saw how such divisions were based on falsehood and hypocrisies, and how they degraded every level of society.

So, when the Revd Lindley comes to the poor parish of Aldecross 'to live on a stipend of about a hundred and twenty pounds', he is scarcely better off than 'the new, raw, disaffected population of colliers' but must 'keep up a superior position' and 'has no doubts of himself'. They have no respect for him, however: taking umbrage at his comment on her hard-drinking son, a woman snaps back, '"And why indeed shouldn't he have his glass?... He picks no man's pocket to pay for it." The clergyman stiffened at what he thought was an allusion to his own profession, and his unpaid bills.' The church too is divided, into high and low. '"Oh, it's no good you coming here," a woman tells him, "'we're chapel."' And in this early story there is already the tension within Lawrence between what is regarded as the narrowness and rigidity of the Christian Church and the appeal of paganism, with its liberating acceptance of all the contradictions within human nature. Also his ideas of the separate aspects of masculine and feminine nature, of the primal purity of each, and at the same time their interdependence, essential if men and women were to achieve their full potential.

Lawrence plays the role of the observer in the corner, the outsider with the dark, brooding presence, watching – chin in hand and brow lowered – the cast of characters he has set amidst the stage sets, a vicarage and a collier's cottage. At the vicarage they are the haughty, contemptuous Revd Lindley; his once spirited and self-assured wife, driven by their mean, penny-pinching existence to her sickbed and an evil disposition; their two daughters – Mary, who is beautiful, proud and never allows a feeling or an impulse to get the better of her principles, and Louisa, who is short and stout and ruled by her passions; and Mr Massy, who comes to the vicarage to help when the vicar is ill, 'spectacled, timid in the extreme... yet with a certain inhuman self-sureness' and becomes Miss Mary's somewhat repulsive suitor ('her physical self disliked and despised him. But she was in the grip of his moral, mental being'). Down in the cottage below the railway line lies the collier, ill and dying, while his wife rails against life's injustices – in this case, her favourite son Alfred's volunteering to serve in the Navy. The two households are set against each other by the socially unacceptable attraction between Miss Louisa and Alfred, providing Lawrence with the clash of character, type and class that he needs to light a fire in his fiction.

Lawrence needed light – candlelight, firelight, the light on a field of snow – in the years before he discovered Italian and Mexican skies, to warm him into a state where he could provide portrayal to his theories. One can grow impatient with them, of the way he watches and comments, and one can laugh, nowadays, at the scenes of physical passion that in his day must have seemed shocking ('he put his arms round her, and took her, cruelly, blindly, straining her till she almost lost consciousness, till he himself had almost fallen,' and she 'yielded up, swooned to a kind of death of herself, a moment of utter darkness came over him, and they began to wake up again as if from a long sleep'), but one cannot deny the intensity he generates, and how extraordinary, and groundbreaking his language was in 1911.

Then, when he manages to put aside his theories and analyses, and allows his characters to come to life as more than the types they represent, his fiction acquires a momentum, his characters breaking out from the iron grip of his control and showing themselves to be creatures of flesh and blood, capable of surprising us – and themselves. And it is not only people, it is every object, animate and inanimate, on which he focuses his attention that stirs to life in response. Even a stone church, the church at Aldecross, for instance, with its 'uncertain, timid look' takes on an existence that is almost sentient: 'the little building crouched like a humped stone-and-mortar mouse, with two little turrets at the west corner for ears'.

There are many touches, too, of the tenderness and lyricism so prominent in his poetry – the collier's cottage in 'a quiet little underworld of its own' with snowdrops 'hanging very still under the bare currant bushes', or the hills covered with 'silent blue snow'. Every glimpse of the outer, natural world comes as if upon a sweet, vernal breeze. Houses – the vicarage and the collier's cottage – are, by contrast, as dark and stifling as prisons. That is where lives are mostly lived in a cold climate of course, circumscribed and mostly circumspect, but there are scenes of great sweetness and tenderness, as when Mary takes her children to visit the vicarage:

> ' "Oh a pretty! – a little pretty! Oh a cold little pretty come in a railway-train!" Miss Louisa was cooing to the infant, crouching on the hearthrug… the mother, coming and closing her hand judiciously over the rosy feet and hands of the mite.'

The short journey itself, by train through darkness and snowfall, is rendered with all the excitement felt by young Jack, scrambling from one seat to another so as to miss none of the flying snowflakes.

There we have the D.H. Lawrence of his youth, of our

youth too, and the youth of the twentieth century. He was to go far, far beyond that, but here, in the little story, *Daughters of the Vicar* (could any title be more redolent of the England of its time?) we have the essential D.H. Lawrence – the little contained world in a mossy valley of coal-veined hills from which *that* D.H. Lawrence grew.

– Anita Desai, 2004

Daughters of the Vicar

CHAPTER ONE

Mr Lindley was the first vicar of Aldecross. The cottages of this tiny hamlet had nestled in peace since their beginning, and the country folk had crossed the lanes and farmlands, two or three miles, to the parish church at Greymeed, on the bright Sunday mornings.

But when the pits were sunk, blank rows of dwellings started up beside the high roads, and a new population, skimmed from the floating scum of workmen, was filled in, the cottages and the country people were almost obliterated.

To suit the convenience of these new collier-inhabitants, a church must be built at Aldecross. There was not too much money. And so the little building crouched like a humped stone-and-mortar mouse, with two little turrets at the west corner for ears, in the fields near the cottages and the apple trees, as far as possible from the dwellings down the high road. It had an uncertain, timid look about it. And so they planted big-leaved ivy to hide its shrinking newness. So that now the little church stands, buried in its greenery, stranded and sleeping among the fields, while the brick houses elbow nearer and nearer, threatening to crush it down. It is already obsolete.

The Revd Ernest Lindley, aged twenty-seven, and newly married, came from his curacy in Suffolk to take charge of his church. He was just an ordinary young man, who had been to Cambridge and taken orders. His wife was a self-assured young woman, daughter of a Cambridgeshire rector. Her father had spent the whole of his thousand a year, so that Mrs Lindley had nothing to her own. Thus the young married people came to Aldecross to live on a stipend of about a hundred and twenty pounds, and to keep up a superior position.

3

They were not very well received by the new, raw, disaffected population of colliers. Being accustomed to farm labourers, Mr Lindley had considered himself as belonging indisputably to the upper or ordering classes. He had to be humble to the country families, but still, he was of their kind, whilst the common people were something different. He had no doubts of himself.

He found, however, that the collier population refused to accept this arrangement. They had no use for him in their lives, and they told him so, callously. The women merely said, 'they were throng', or else, 'Oh, it's no good you coming here, we're chapel.' The men were quite good-humoured so long as he did not touch them too nigh, they were cheerfully contemptuous of him, with a preconceived contempt he was powerless against.

At last, passing from indignation to silent resentment, even, if he dared have acknowledged it, to conscious hatred of the majority of his flock, and unconscious hatred of himself, he confined his activities to a narrow round of cottages, and he had to submit. He had no particular character, having always depended on his position in society to give him position among men. Now he was so poor, he had no social standing even among the common vulgar tradespeople of the district, and he had not the nature nor the wish to make his society agreeable to them, nor the strength to impose himself where he would have liked to be recognised. He dragged on, pale and miserable and neutral.

At first his wife raged with mortification. She took on airs and used a high hand. But her income was too small, the wrestling with tradesmen's bills was too pitiful, she only met with general, callous ridicule when she tried to be impressive.

Wounded to the quick of her pride, she found herself

isolated in an indifferent, callous population. She raged indoors and out. But soon she learnt that she must pay too heavily for her outdoor rages, and then she only raged within the walls of the rectory. There her feeling was so strong that she frightened herself. She saw herself hating her husband, and she knew that, unless she were careful, she would smash her form of life and bring catastrophe upon him and upon herself. So in very fear she went quiet. She hid, bitter and beaten by fear, behind the only shelter she had in the world, her gloomy, poor parsonage.

Children were born one every year; almost mechanically, she continued to perform her maternal duty, which was forced upon her. Gradually, broken by the suppressing of her violent anger and misery and disgust, she became an invalid and took to her couch.

The children grew up healthy, but unwarmed and rather rigid. Their father and mother educated them at home, made them very proud and very genteel, put them definitely and cruelly in the upper classes, apart from the vulgar around them. So they lived quite isolated. They were good-looking, and had that curiously clean, semi-transparent look of the genteel, isolated poor.

Gradually Mr and Mrs Lindley lost all hold on life, and spent their hours, weeks and years merely haggling to make ends meet, and bitterly repressing and pruning their children into gentility, urging them to ambition, weighing them with duty. On Sunday morning the whole family, except the mother, went down the lane to church, the long-legged girls in skimpy frocks, the boys in black coats, and long, grey unfitting trousers. They passed by their father's parishioners with mute, clear faces, childish mouths closed in pride that was like a doom to them, and childish eyes already unseeing. Miss

5

Mary, the eldest, was the leader. She was a long, slim thing with a fine profile and a proud, pure look of submission to a high fate. Miss Louisa, the second, was short and plump and obstinate-looking. She had more enemies than ideals. She looked after the lesser children, Miss Mary after the elder. The collier children watched this pale, distinguished profession of the vicar's family pass by, and they were impressed by the air of gentility and distance, they made mock of the trousers of the small sons, they felt inferior in themselves, and hate stirred their hearts.

In her time, Miss Mary received as governess a few little daughters of tradesmen; Miss Louisa managed the house and went among her father's churchgoers, giving lessons on the piano to the collier's daughters at thirteen shillings for twenty-six lessons.

CHAPTER TWO

One winter morning, when his daughter Mary was about twenty years old, Mr Lindley, a thin, unobtrusive figure in his black overcoat and his wide-awake, went down into Aldecross with a packet of white papers under his arm. He was delivering the parish almanacs.

A rather pale, neutral man of middle age, he waited while the train thumped over the level crossing, going up to the pit which rattled busily just along the line. A wooden-legged man hobbled to open the gate. Mr Lindley passed on. Just at his left hand, below the road and the railway, was the red roof of a cottage, showing through the bare twigs of apple trees. Mr Lindley passed round the low wall, and descended the worn steps that led from the highway down to the cottage which crouched darkly and quietly away below the rumble of passing trains and the clank of coal-carts, in a quiet little underworld of its own. Snowdrops with tight-shut buds were hanging very still under the bare currant bushes.

The clergyman was just going to knock when he heard a clinking noise, and, turning, saw through the open door of a black shed just behind him an elderly woman in a black lace cap stooping among reddish big cans, pouring a very bright liquid into a tundish. There was a smell of paraffin. The woman put down the can, took the tundish and laid it on a shelf, then rose with a tin bottle. Her eyes met those of the clergyman.

'Oh, is it you, Mr Lin'ley!' she said, in a complaining tone. 'Go in.'

The minister entered the house. In the hot kitchen sat a big, elderly man with a great grey beard, taking snuff. He grunted in a deep, muttering voice, telling the minister to sit down, and then took no more notice of him, but stared vacantly into the fire. Mr Lindley waited.

The woman came in, the ribbons of her black lace cap, or bonnet, hanging on her shawl. She was of medium stature, everything about her was tidy. She went up a step out of the kitchen, carrying a paraffin tin. Feet were heard entering the room up the step. It was a little haberdashery shop, with parcels on the shelves of the walls, a big, old-fashioned sewing machine with tailor's work lying round it, in the open space. The woman went behind the counter, gave the child who had entered the paraffin bottle, and took from her a jug.

'My mother says shall yer put it down,' said the child, and she was gone. The woman wrote in a book, then came into the kitchen with her jug. The husband, a very large man, rose and brought more coal to the already hot fire. He moved slowly and sluggishly. Already he was going dead; being a tailor, his large form had become an encumbrance to him. In his youth he had been a great dancer and boxer. Now he was taciturn, and inert. The minister had nothing to say, so he sought for his phrases. But John Durant took no notice, existing silent and dull.

Mrs Durant spread the cloth. Her husband poured himself beer into a mug, and began to smoke and drink.

'Shall you have some?' he growled through his beard at the clergyman, looking slowly from the man to the jug, capable of this one idea.

'No, thank you,' replied Lindley, though he would have liked some beer. He must set an example in a drinking parish.

'We need a drop to keep us going,' said Mrs Durant.

She had rather a complaining manner. The clergyman sat on uncomfortably while she laid the table for the half-past ten lunch. Her husband drew up to eat. She remained in her little round armchair by the fire.

She was a woman who would have liked to be easy in her life, but to whose lot had fallen a rough and turbulent family, and a slothful husband who did not care what became of himself or anybody. So, her rather good-looking square face was peevish, she had that air of having been compelled all her life to serve unwillingly, and to control what she did not want to control. There was about her, too, that masterful aplomb of a woman who has brought up and ruled her sons: but even them she had ruled unwillingly. She had enjoyed managing her little haberdashery shop, riding in the carrier's cart to Nottingham, going through the big warehouses to buy her goods. But the fret of managing her sons she did not like. Only she loved her youngest boy, because he was her last, and she saw herself free.

This was one of the houses the clergyman visited occasionally. Mrs Durant, as part of her regulation, had brought up all her sons in the Church. Not that she had any religion. Only, it was what she was used to do. Mr Durant was without religion. He read the fervently evangelical *Life of John Wesley* with a curious pleasure, getting from it a satisfaction as from the warmth of the fire or a glass of brandy. But he cared no more about John Wesley, in fact, than about John Milton, of whom he had never heard.

Mrs Durant took her chair to the table.

'I don't feel like eating,' she sighed.

'Why – aren't you well?' asked the clergyman, patronising.

'It isn't that,' she sighed. She sat with a shut, straight mouth. 'I don't know what's going to become of us.'

But the clergyman had ground himself down so long that he could not easily sympathise.

'Have you any trouble?' he asked.

9

'Ay, have I any trouble!' cried the elderly woman. 'I shall end my days in the workhouse.'

The minister waited unmoved. What could she know of poverty, in her little house of plenty?

'I hope not,' he said.

'And the one lad as I wanted to keep by me –' she lamented.

The minister listened without sympathy, quite neutral.

'And the lad as would have been a support to my old age! What is going to become of us?' she said.

The clergyman, justly, did not believe in the cry of poverty, but wondered what had become of the son.

'Has anything happened to Alfred?' he asked.

'We've got word he's gone for a Queen's sailor,' she said sharply.

'He has joined the Navy!' exclaimed Mr Lindley. 'I think he could scarcely have done better – to serve his Queen and country on the sea…'

'He is wanted to serve *me*,' she cried. 'And I wanted my lad at home.'

Alfred was her baby, her last, whom she had allowed herself the luxury of spoiling.

'You will miss him,' said Mr Lindley, 'that is certain. But this is no regrettable step for him to have taken – on the contrary.'

'That's easy for you to say, Mr Lindley,' she replied tartly. 'Do you think I want my lad climbing ropes at another man's bidding, like a monkey –?'

'There is no *dishonour*, surely, in serving in the Navy?'

'Dishonour this, dishonour that,' cried the angry old woman. 'He goes and makes a slave of himself, and he'll rue it.'

Her angry, scornful impatience nettled the clergyman, and silenced him for some moments.

'I do not see,' he retorted at last, white at the gills and

inadequate, 'that the Queen's service is any more to be called slavery than working in a mine.'

'At home he was at home, and his own master. *I* know he'll find a difference.'

'It may be the making of him,' said the clergyman. 'It will take him away from bad companionship and drink.'

Some of the Durants' sons were notorious drinkers, and Alfred was not quite steady.

'And why indeed shouldn't he have his glass?' cried the mother. 'He picks no man's pocket to pay for it!'

The clergyman stiffened at what he thought was an allusion to his own profession, and his unpaid bills.

'With all due consideration, I am glad to hear he has joined the Navy,' he said.

'Me with my old age coming on, and his father working very little! I'd thank you to be glad about something else besides that, Mr Lindley.'

The woman began to cry. Her husband, quite impassive, finished his lunch of meat pie, and drank some beer. Then he turned to the fire, as if there were no one in the room but himself.

'I shall respect all men who serve God and their country on the sea, Mrs Durant,' said the clergyman stubbornly.

'That is very well, when they're not your sons who are doing the dirty work. It makes a difference,' she replied tartly.

'I should be proud if one of my sons were to enter the Navy.'

'Ay – well – we're not all of us made alike –'

The minister rose. He put down a large folded paper.

'I've brought the almanac,' he said.

Mrs Durant unfolded it.

'I do like a bit of colour in things,' she said, petulantly.

The clergyman did not reply.

'There's that envelope for the organist's fund –' said the old woman, and rising, she took the thing from the mantelpiece, went into the shop, and returned sealing it up.

'Which is all I can afford,' she said.

Mr Lindley took his departure, and in his pocket the envelope containing Mrs Durrant's offering for Miss Louisa's services. He went from door to door delivering the almanacs, in dull routine. Jaded with the monotony of the business, and with the repeated effort of greeting half-known people, he felt barren and rather irritable. At last he returned home.

In the dining room was a small fire. Mrs Lindley, growing very stout, lay on her couch. The vicar carved the cold mutton; Miss Louisa, short and plump and rather flushed, came in from the kitchen; Miss Mary, dark, with a beautiful white brow and grey eyes, served the vegetables; the children chattered a little, but not exuberantly. The air seemed starved.

'I went to the Durants,' said the vicar, as he served out small portions of mutton; 'it appears Alfred has run away to join the Navy.'

'Do him good,' came the rough voice of the invalid.

Miss Louisa, attending to the youngest child, looked up in protest.

'Why has he done that?' asked Mary's low, musical voice.

'He wanted some excitement, I suppose,' said the vicar. 'Shall we say grace?'

The children were arranged, all bent their heads, grace was pronounced, at the last word every face was being raised to go on with the interesting subject.

'He's just done the right thing, for once,' came the rather deep voice of the mother; 'save him from becoming a drunken sot, like the rest of them.'

'They're not *all* drunken, Mama,' said Miss Louisa, stubbornly.

'It's no fault of their upbringing if they're not. Walter Durant is a standing disgrace.'

'As I told Mrs Durant,' said the vicar, eating hungrily, 'it is the best thing he could have done. It will take him away from temptation during the most dangerous years of his life – how old is he – nineteen?'

'Twenty,' said Miss Louisa.

'Twenty!' repeated the vicar. 'It will give him wholesome discipline and set before him some standard of duty and honour – nothing could have been better for him. But –'

'We shall miss him from the choir,' said Miss Louisa, as if taking opposite sides to her parents.

'That is as may be,' said the vicar. 'I prefer to know he is safe in the Navy than running the risk of getting into bad ways here.'

'Was he getting into bad ways?' asked the stubborn Miss Louisa.

'You know, Louisa, he wasn't quite what he used to be,' said Miss Mary gently and steadily. Miss Louisa shut her rather heavy jaw sulkily. She wanted to deny it, but she knew it was true.

For her he had been a laughing, warm lad, with something kindly and something rich about him. He had made her feel warm. It seemed the days would be colder since he had gone.

'Quite the best thing he could do,' said the mother with emphasis.

'I think so,' said the vicar. 'But his mother was almost abusive because I suggested it.'

He spoke in an injured tone.

'What does she care for her children's welfare?' said the

invalid. 'Their wages is all her concern.'

'I suppose she wanted him at home with her,' said Miss Louisa.

'Yes, she did – at the expense of his learning to be a drunkard like the rest of them,' retorted her mother.

'George Durant doesn't drink,' defended her daughter.

'Because he got burnt so badly when he was nineteen – in the pit – and that frightened him. The Navy is a better remedy than that, at least.'

'Certainly,' said the vicar. 'Certainly.'

And to this Miss Louisa agreed. Yet she could not but feel angry that he had gone away for so many years. She herself was only nineteen.

CHAPTER THREE

It happened when Miss Mary was twenty-three years old that Mr Lindley was very ill. The family was exceedingly poor at the time, such a lot of money was needed, so little was forthcoming. Neither Miss Mary nor Miss Louisa had suitors. What chance had they? They met no eligible men in Aldecross. And what they earned was a mere drop in a void. The girls' hearts were chilled and hardened with fear of this perpetual, cold penury, this narrow struggle, this horrible nothingness of their lives.

A clergyman had to be found for the church work. It so happened that the son of an old friend of Mr Lindley's was waiting three months before taking up his duties. He would come and officiate, for nothing. The young clergyman was keenly expected. He was not more than twenty-seven, a Master of Arts of Oxford, had written his thesis on Roman law. He came of an old Cambridgeshire family, had some private means, was going to take a church in Northamptonshire with a good stipend, and was not married. Mrs Lindley incurred new debts, and scarcely regretted her husband's illness.

But when Mr Massy came there was a shock of disappointment in the house. They had expected a young man with a pipe and a deep voice, but with better manners than Sidney, the eldest of the Lindleys. There arrived instead a small, *chétif* man, scarcely larger than a boy of twelve, spectacled, timid in the extreme, without a word to utter at first; yet with a certain inhuman self-sureness.

'What a little abortion!' was Mrs Lindley's exclamation to herself on first seeing him, in his buttoned-up clerical coat. And for the first time for many days she was profoundly thankful to God that all her children were decent specimens.

He had not normal powers of perception. They soon saw that he lacked the full range of human feelings, but had rather a strong, philosophical mind, from which he lived. His body was almost unthinkable, in intellect he was something definite. The conversation at once took a balanced, abstract tone, when he participated. There was no spontaneous exclamation, no violent assertion or expression of personal conviction, but all cold, reasonable assertion. This was very hard on Mrs Lindley. The little man would look at her, after one of her pronouncements, and then give, in his thin voice, his own calculated version, so that she felt as if she were tumbling into thin air through a hole in the flimsy floor on which their conversation stood. It was she who felt a fool. Soon she was reduced to a hardy silence.

Still, at the back of her mind, she remembered that he was an unattached gentleman, who would shortly have an income altogether of six or seven hundred a year. What did the man matter, if there were pecuniary ease! The man was a trifle thrown in. After twenty-two years her sentimentality was ground away, and only the millstone of poverty mattered to her. So she supported the little man as a representative of a decent income.

His most irritating habit was that of a sneering little giggle, all on his own, which came when he perceived or related some logical absurdity on the part of another person. It was the only form of humour he had. Stupidity in thinking seemed to him exquisitely funny. But any novel was unintelligibly meaningless and dull, and to an Irish sort of humour he listened curiously, examining it like mathematics, or else simply not hearing. In normal human relationship he was not there. Quite unable to take part in simple everyday talk, he padded silently round the house, or sat in the dining room looking nervously from side to side, always apart in a cold, rarefied little world of his own. Sometimes he made an ironic remark that did not seem humanly relevant, or he gave his little laugh, like a sneer. He had to defend himself and his own insufficiency. And he answered questions grudgingly, with a yes or no, because he did not see their import and was nervous. It seemed to Miss Louisa he scarcely distinguished one person from another, but that he liked to be near to her, or to Miss Mary, for some sort of contact which stimulated him unknown.

Apart from all this, he was the most admirable workman. He was unremittingly shy, but perfect in his sense of duty: as far as he could conceive Christianity, he was a perfect Christian. Nothing that he realised he could do for anyone did he leave undone. Although he was so incapable of coming into contact with another being that he could not proffer help. Now he attended assiduously to the sick man, investigated all the affairs of the parish or the church which Mr Lindley had in control, straightened out accounts, made lists of the sick and needy, padded round with help and to see what he could do. He heard of Mrs Lindley's anxiety about her sons, and began to investigate means of sending them to Cambridge. His kindness almost frightened Miss Mary. She honoured it so, and yet she shrank from it. For, in it all Mr Massy seemed to have no sense of any person, any human being whom he was helping: he only realised a kind of mathematical working out, solving of given situations, a calculated well-doing. And it was as if he had accepted the Christian tenets as axioms. His religion consisted in what his scrupulous abstract mind approved of.

Seeing his acts, Miss Mary must respect and honour him. In consequence she must serve him. To this she had to force herself, shuddering and yet desirous, but he did not perceive it. She accompanied him on his visiting in the parish, and whilst she was cold with admiration for him, often she was touched with pity for the little paddling figure with bent shoulders, buttoned up to the chin in his overcoat. She was a handsome, calm girl, tall, with a beautiful repose. Her clothes were poor, and she wore a black scarf, having no furs. But she was a lady. As the people saw her walking down Aldecross beside Mr Massy they said:

'My word, Miss Mary's got a catch. Did you ever see such a sickly little shrimp!'

She knew they were talking so, and it made her heart grow hot against them, and she drew herself as it were protectively towards the little man beside her. At any rate, she could see and give honour to his genuine goodness.

He could not walk fast, or far.

'You have not been well?' she asked in her dignified way.

'I have an internal trouble.'

He was not aware of her slight shudder. There was silence, whilst she bowed to recover her composure, to resume her gentle manner towards him.

He was fond of Miss Mary. She had made it a rule of hospitality that he should always be escorted by herself or by her sister on his visits in the parish, which were not many. But some mornings she was engaged. It was no good Miss Louisa's trying to adopt to Mr Massy an attitude of queenly service. She was unable to regard him save with aversion. When she saw him from behind, thin and bent-shouldered, looking like a sickly lad of thirteen, she disliked him exceedingly, and felt a desire to put him out of existence. And yet a deeper justice in Mary made Louisa humble before her sister.

They were going to see Mr Durant, who was paralysed and

not expected to live. Miss Louisa was cruelly ashamed at being admitted to the cottage in company with the little clergyman.

Mrs Durant was, however, much quieter in the face of her real trouble.

'How is Mr Durant?' asked Louisa.

'He is no different – and we don't expect him to be,' was the reply. The little clergyman stood looking on.

They went upstairs. The three stood for some time looking at the bed, and the grey head of the old man on the pillow, the grey beard over the sheet. Miss Louisa was shocked and afraid.

'It is so dreadful,' she said, with a shudder.

'It is how I always thought it would be,' replied Mrs Durant.

Then Miss Louisa was afraid of her. The two women were uneasy, waiting for Mr Massy to say something. He stood, small and bent, too nervous to speak.

'Has he any understanding?' he asked at length.

'Maybe?' said Mrs Durant. 'Can you hear, John?' he asked loudly. The dull blue eye of the inert man looked at her feebly.

'Yes, he understands,' said Mrs Durant to Mr Massy. Except for the dull look in his eyes, the sick man lay as if dead. The three stood in silence. Miss Louisa was obstinate but heavy-hearted under the load of unlivingness. It was Mr Massy who kept her there in discipline. His non-human will dominated them all.

Then they heard a sound below, a man's footsteps, and a man's voice called subduedly:

'Are you upstairs, Mother?'

Mrs Durant started and moved to the door. But already a quick, firm step was running up the stairs.

'I'm a bit early, Mother,' a troubled voice said, and on the landing they saw the form of the sailor. His mother came and clung to him. She was suddenly aware that she needed something to hold on to. He put his arms round her, and bent over her, kissing her.

'He's not gone, Mother?' he asked anxiously, struggling to control his voice.

Miss Louisa looked away from the mother and son who stood together on the landing. They could not bear it that she and Mr Massy should be there. The latter stood nervously as if ill at ease before the emotion that was running. He was a witness nervous, unwilling, but dispassionate. To Louisa's hot heart it seemed all, all wrong that they should be there.

Mrs Durant entered the bedroom, her face wet.

'There's Miss Louisa and the vicar,' she said, out of voice and quavering.

Her son, red-faced and slender, drew himself up to salute. But Miss Louisa held out her hand. Then she saw his hazel eyes recognise her for a moment, and his small white teeth showed in a glimpse of the greeting she used to love. She was covered with confusion. He went round to the bed; his boots clicked on the plaster floor, he bowed his head with dignity.

'How are you, Dad?' he said, laying his hand on the sheet, faltering. But the old man stared fixedly and unseeing. The son stood perfectly still for a few minutes, then slowly recoiled. Miss Louisa saw the fine outline of his breast, under the sailor's blue blouse, as his chest began to heave.

'He doesn't know me,' he said, turning to his mother. He gradually went white.

'No, my boy!' cried the mother, pitiful, lifting her face. And suddenly she put her face against his shoulder, he was stooping down to her, holding her against him, and she cried aloud for a moment or two. Miss Louisa saw his sides heaving, and heard the sharp hiss of his breath. She turned away, tears streaming down her face. The father lay inert upon the white bed, Mr Massy looked queer and obliterated, so little now that the sailor with his sunburned skin was in the room. He stood waiting. Miss Louisa wanted to die, she wanted to have done. She dared not turn round again to look.

'Shall I offer a prayer?' came the frail voice of the clergyman, and all kneeled down.

Miss Louisa was frightened of the inert man upon the bed. Then she felt a flash of fear of Mr Massy, hearing his thin, detached voice. And then, calmed, she looked up. On the far side of the bed were the heads of mother and son, the one on the black lace cap, and the small white nape of the neck beneath, the other, with brown, sun-scorched hair too close and wiry to allow of a parting, and neck tanned firm, bowed as if unwillingly. The great grey beard of the old man did not move, the prayer continued. Mr Massy prayed with a pure lucidity that they all might conform to the higher Will. He was like something that dominated the bowed heads, something dispassionate that governed them inexorably. Miss Louisa was afraid of him. And she was bound, during the course of the prayer, to have a little reverence for him. It was like a foretaste of inexorable, cold death, a taste of pure justice.

That evening she talked to Mary of the visit. Her heart, her veins were possessed by the thought of Alfred Durant as he held his mother in his arms; then the break in his voice, as she remembered it again and again, was like a flame through her; and she wanted to see his face more distinctly in her mind, ruddy with the sun, and his golden-brown eyes, kind and careless, strained now with a natural fear, the fine nose tanned hard by the sun, the mouth that could not help smiling at her. And it went through her with pride, to think of his figure, a straight, fine jet of life.

'He is a handsome lad,' said she to Miss Mary, as if he had not been a year older than herself. Underneath was the deeper dread, almost hatred, of the inhuman being of Mr Massy. She felt she must protect herself and Mr Massy from him.

'When I felt Mr Massy there,' she said, 'I almost hated him. What right had he to be there!'

'Surely he had all right,' said Miss Mary after a pause. 'He is *really* a Christian.'

'He seems to me nearly an imbecile,' said Miss Louisa.

Miss Mary, quiet and beautiful, was silent for a moment:

'Oh, no,' she said. 'Not *imbecile* –'

'Well then – he reminds me of a six months' child – or a five months' child – as if he didn't have time to get developed enough before he was born.'

'Yes,' said Miss Mary, slowly. 'There is something lacking. But there is something wonderful in him: and he is really *good* –'

'Yes,' said Miss Louisa, 'it doesn't seem right that he should be. What right has *that* to be called goodness!'

'But it *is* goodness,' persisted Mary. Then she added, with a laugh: 'And come, you wouldn't deny that as well.'

There was a doggedness in her voice. She went about very quietly. In her soul, she knew what was going to happen. She knew that Mr Massy was stronger than she, and that she must submit to what he was. Her physical self was prouder, stronger than he, her physical self disliked and despised him. But she was in the grip of his moral, mental being. And she felt the days allotted out to her. And her family watched.

CHAPTER FOUR

A few days after, old Mr Durant died. Miss Louisa saw Alfred once more, but he was stiff before her now, treating her not like a person, but as if she were some sort of will in command and he a separate, distinct will waiting in front of her. She had never felt such utter steel-plate separation from anyone. It puzzled her and frightened her. What had become of him? And she hated the military discipline – she was antagonistic to it. Now he was not himself. He was the will which obeys set over against the will which commands. She hesitated over accepting this. He had put himself out of her range. He had ranked himself inferior, subordinate to her. And that was how he would get away from her, that was how he would avoid all connection with her: by fronting her impersonally from the opposite camp, by taking up the abstract position of an inferior.

She was brooding steadily and sullenly over this, brooding and brooding. Her fierce, obstinate heart could not give way. It clung to its own rights. Sometimes she dismissed him. Why should he, her inferior, trouble her?

Then she relapsed to him, and almost hated him. It was his way of getting out of it. She felt the cowardice of it, his calmly putting her in a superior class, and placing himself inaccessibly apart, in an inferior, as if she, the sentient woman who was fond of him, did not count. But she was not going to submit. Dogged in her heart, she held onto him.

CHAPTER FIVE

In six months' time Miss Mary had married Mr Massy. There had been no love-making, nobody had made any remark. But everybody was tense and callous with expectation. When one day Mr Massy asked for Mary's hand, Mr Lindley started and trembled from the thin, abstract voice of the little man. Mr Massy was very nervous, but so curiously absolute.

'I shall be very glad,' said the vicar, 'but of course the decision lies with Mary herself.' And his still feeble hand shook as he moved a Bible on his desk.

The small man, keeping fixedly to his idea, padded out of the room to find Miss Mary. He sat a long time by her, while she made some conversation, before he had readiness to speak. She was afraid of what was coming, and sat stiff in apprehension. She felt as if her body would rise and fling him aside. But her spirit quivered and waited. Almost in expectation she waited, almost wanting him. And then she knew he would speak.

'I have already asked Mr Lindley,' said the clergyman, while suddenly she looked with aversion at his little knees, 'if he would consent to my proposal.' He was aware of his own disadvantage, but his will was set.

She went cold as she sat, and impervious, almost as if she had become stone. He waited a moment nervously. He would not persuade her. He himself never even heard persuasion but pursued his own course. He looked at her, sure of himself, unsure of her, and said:

'Will you become my wife, Mary?'

Still her heart was hard and cold. She sat proudly.

'I should like to speak to Mama first,' she said.

'Very well,' replied Mr Massy. And in a moment he padded away.

Mary went to her mother. She was cold and reserved.

'Mr Massy has asked me to marry him, Mama,' she said. Mrs Lindley went on staring at her book. She was cramped in her feeling.

'Well, and what did you say?'

They were both keeping calm and cold.

'I said I would speak to you before answering him.'

This was equivalent to a question. Mrs Lindley did not want to reply to it. She shifted her heavy form irritably on the couch. Miss Mary sat calm and straight, with closed mouth.

'Your father thinks it would not be a bad match,' said the mother, as if casually.

Nothing more was said. Everybody remained cold and shut off. Miss Mary did not speak to Miss Louisa, the Revd Ernest Lindley kept out of sight.

At evening Miss Mary accepted Mr Massy.

'Yes, I will marry you,' she said, with even a little movement of tenderness towards him. He was embarrassed, but satisfied. She could see him making some movement towards her, could feel the male in him, something cold and triumphant, asserting herself. She sat rigid, and waited.

When Miss Louisa knew, she was silent with bitter anger against everybody, even against Mary. She felt her faith wounded. Did the real thing to her not matter after all? She wanted to get away. She thought of Mr Massy. He had some curious power, some unanswerable right. He was a will that they could not controvert. Suddenly a flush started in her. If he had come to her she would have flipped him out of the room. He was never going to touch *her*. And she was glad. She was glad that her blood would rise and exterminate the little man, if he came too near to her, no matter how her judgement was paralysed by him, no matter how he moved in abstract goodness. She thought she was perverse to be glad, but glad she was. 'I would just flip him out of the room,' she said, and she derived great satisfaction from the open statement. Nevertheless, perhaps she ought still to feel that Mary, on her plane, was a higher being than herself. But then Mary was Mary, and she was Louisa, and that also was unalterable.

Mary, in marrying him, tried to become a pure reason such as he was, without feeling or impulse. She shut herself up, she shut herself rigid against the agonies of shame and the terror of violation which came at first. She *would* not feel, and she *would* not feel. She was a pure will acquiescing to him. She elected a certain kind of fate. She would be good and purely just, she would live in a higher freedom than she had ever known, and would be free of mundane care, she was a pure will towards right. She had sold herself, but she had a new freedom. She had got rid of her body. She had sold a lower thing, her body, for a higher thing, her freedom from material things. She considered that she paid for all she got from her husband. So, in a kind of independence, she moved proud and free. She had paid with her body: that was henceforward out of consideration. She was glad to be rid of it. She had bought her position in the world – that henceforth was taken for granted. There remained only the direction of her activity towards charity and high-minded living.

She could scarcely bear other people to be present with her and her husband. Her private life was her shame. But then, she could keep it hidden. She lived almost isolated in the rectory of the tiny village miles from the railway. She suffered as if it were an insult to her own flesh, seeing the repulsion which some people felt for her husband, or the special manner they had of treating him, as if he were a 'case'. But most people were uneasy before him, which restored her pride.

If she had let herself, she would have hated him, hated his padding round the house, his thin voice devoid of human understanding, his bent little shoulders and rather incomplete face that reminded her of an abortion. But rigorously she kept to her position. She took care of him and was just to him. There was also a deep, craven fear of him, something slave-like.

There was not much fault to he found with his behaviour. He was scrupulously just and kind according to his lights. But the male in him was cold and self-complete, and utterly domineering. Weak, insufficient little thing as he was, she had not expected this of him. It was something in the bargain she had not understood. It made her hold her head, to keep still. She knew, vaguely, that she was murdering herself. After all, her body was not quite so easy to get rid of. And this manner of disposing of it – ah, sometimes she felt she must rise and bring about death, lift her hand for utter denial of everything, but a general destruction.

He was almost unaware of the conditions about him. He did not fuss in the domestic way, she did as she liked in the house. Indeed, she was a great deal free of him. He would sit obliterated for hours. He was kind, and almost anxiously considerate. But when he considered he was right, his will was just blindly male, like a cold machine. And on most points he was logically right, or he had with him the right of the creed they both accepted. It was so. There was nothing for her to go against.

Then she found herself with child, and felt for the first time horror, afraid before God and man. This also she had to go through – it was the right. When the child arrived, it was a bonny, healthy lad. Her head hurt in her body as she took the baby between her hands. The flesh that was trampled and silent in her must speak again in the boy. After all, she had to live – it was not so simple after all. Nothing was finished completely. She looked and looked at the baby, and almost hated it, and suffered an anguish of love for it. She hated it because it made her live again in the flesh, when she *could* not live in the flesh, she could not. She wanted to trample her flesh down, down, extinct, to live in the mind. And now there was this child. It was too cruel, too racking. For she must love the child. Her purpose was broken in two again. She had to become amorphous, purposeless, without real being. As a mother, she was a fragmentary, ignoble thing.

Mr Massy, blind to everything else in the way of human feeling, became obsessed by the idea of his child. When it arrived, suddenly it filled the whole world of feeling for him. It was his obsession, his terror was for its safety and well-being. It was something new, as if he himself had been born a naked infant, conscious of his own exposure, and full of apprehension. He who had never been aware of anyone else, all his life, now was aware of nothing but the child. Not that he ever played with it, or kissed it, or tended it. He did nothing for it. But it dominated him, it filled, and at the same time emptied his mind. The world was all baby for him.

This his wife must also bear, this question: 'What is the reason that he cries?' – his first reminder, at the first sound: 'Mary, that is the child' – his restlessness if the feeding-time were five minutes past. She had bargained for this – now she must stand by her bargain.

CHAPTER SIX

Miss Louisa, at home in the dingy vicarage, had suffered a great deal over her sister's wedding. Having once begun to cry out against it, during the engagement, she had been silenced by Mary's quiet: 'I don't agree with you about him, Louisa, I *want* to marry him.' Then Miss Louisa had been angry deep in her heart, and therefore silent. This dangerous state started the change in her. Her own revulsion made her recoil from the hitherto undoubted Mary.

'I'd beg the streets barefoot first,' said Miss Louisa, thinking of Mr Massy.

But evidently Mary could perform a different heroism. So she, Louisa the practical, suddenly felt that Mary, her ideal, was questionable after all. How could she be pure – one cannot be dirty in act and spiritual in being. Louisa distrusted Mary's high spirituality. It was no longer genuine for her. And if Mary were spiritual and misguided, why did not her father protect her? Because of the money. And the mother frankly did not care: her daughters could do as they liked. Her mother's pronouncement:

'Whatever happens to *him*, Mary is safe for life,' – so evidently and shallowly a calculation, incensed Louisa.

'I'd rather be safe in the workhouse,' she cried.

'Your father will see to that,' replied her mother brutally. This speech, in its indirectness, so injured Miss Louisa that she hated her mother deep, deep in her heart, and almost hated herself. It was a long time resolving itself out, this hate. But it worked and worked, and at last the young woman said:

'They are wrong – they are all wrong. They have ground out their souls for what isn't worth anything, and there isn't a grain of love in them anywhere. And I *will* have love. They want us to deny it. They've never found it, so they want to say it doesn't exist. But I *will* have it. I *will* love – it is my birthright. I will love the man I marry – that is all I care about.'

So Miss Louisa stood isolated from everybody. She and Mary had parted over Mr Massy. In Louisa's eyes, Mary was degraded, married to Mr Massy. She could not bear to think of her lofty, spiritual sister degraded in the body like this. Mary was wrong, wrong, wrong; she was not superior, she was flawed, incomplete. The two sisters stood apart. They still loved each other, they would love each other as long as they lived. But they had parted ways. A new solitariness came over the obstinate Louisa, and her heavy jaw set stubbornly. She was going on her own way. But which way? She was quite alone, with a blank world before her. How could she be said to have any way? Yet she had her fixed will to love, to have the man she loved.

CHAPTER SEVEN

When her boy was three years old, Mary had another baby, a girl. The three years had gone by monotonously. They might have been an eternity, they might have been brief as a sleep. She did not know. Only, there was always a weight on top of her, something that pressed down her life. The only thing that had happened was that Mr Massy had had an operation. He was always exceedingly fragile. His wife had soon learnt to attend to him mechanically, as part of her duty.

But this third year, after the baby girl had been born, Mary felt oppressed and depressed. Christmas drew near: the gloomy unleavened Christmas of the rectory, where all the days were of the same dark fabric. And Mary was afraid. It was as if the darkness were coming upon her.

'Edward, I should like to go home for Christmas,' she said, and a certain terror filled her as she spoke.

'But you can't leave baby,' said her husband, blinking.

'We can all go.'

He thought, and stared in his collective fashion.

'Why do you wish to go?' he asked.

'Because I need a change. A change would do me good, and it would be good for the milk.'

He heard the will in his wife's voice, and was at a loss. Her language was unintelligible to him. But somehow he felt that Mary was set upon it. And while she was breeding, either about to have a child, or nursing, he regarded her as a special sort of being.

'Wouldn't it hurt baby to take her by the train?' he said.

'No,' replied the mother, 'why should it?'

They went. When they were in the train it began to snow. From the window of his first-class carriage the little clergyman

31

watched the big flakes sweep by, like a blind drawn across the country. He was obsessed by thought of the baby, and afraid of the draughts in the carriage.

'Sit right in the corner,' he said to his wife, 'and hold baby close back.'

She moved at his bidding, and stared out of the window. His eternal presence was like an iron weight on her brain. But she was going partially to escape for a few days.

'Sit on the other side, Jack,' said the father. 'It is less draughty. Come to this window.'

He watched the boy in anxiety. But his children were the only beings in the world who took not the slightest notice of him.

'Look, Mother, look!' cried the boy. 'They fly right in my face' – he meant the snowflakes.

'Come into this corner,' repeated his father, out of another world.

'He's jumped on this one's back, Mother, an' they're riding to the bottom!' cried the boy, jumping with glee.

'Tell him to come on this side,' the little man bade his wife.

'Jack, kneel on this cushion,' said the mother, putting her white hand on the place.

The boy slid over in silence to the place she indicated, waited still for a moment, then almost deliberately, stridently cried: 'Look at all those in the corner, Mother, making a heap,' and he pointed to the cluster of snowflakes with finger pressed dramatically on the pane, and he turned to his mother a bit ostentatiously.

'All in a heap!' she said.

He had seen her face, and had her response, and he was somewhat assured. Vaguely uneasy, he was reassured if he could win her attention.

They arrived at the vicarage at half-past two, not having had lunch.

'How are you, Edward?' said Mr Lindley, trying on his side to be fatherly. But he was always in a false position with his son-in-law, frustrated before him, therefore, as much as possible, he shut his eyes and ears to him. The vicar was looking thin and pale and ill-nourished. He had gone quite grey. He was, however, still haughty; but, since the growing-up of his children, it was a brittle haughtiness, that might break at a moment and leave the vicar only an impoverished, pitiable figure. Mrs Lindley took all the notice of her daughter, and of the children. She ignored her son-in-law. Miss Louisa was clucking and laughing and rejoicing over the baby. Mr Massy stood aside, a bent persistent little figure.

'Oh a pretty! – a little pretty! Oh a cold little pretty come in a railway-train!' Miss Louisa was cooing to the infant, crouching on the hearthrug, opening the white woollen wraps and exposing the child to the fireglow.

'Mary,' said the little clergyman, 'I think it would be better to give baby a warm bath; she may take a cold.'

'I think it is not necessary,' said the mother, coming and closing her hand judiciously over the rosy feet and hands of the mite. 'She is not chilly.'

'Not a bit,' cried Miss Louisa. 'She's not caught cold.'

'I'll go and bring her flannels,' said Mr Massy, with one idea.

'I can bath her in the kitchen then,' said Miss Mary, in an altered, cold tone.

'You can't, the girl is scrubbing there,' said Miss Louisa. 'Besides she doesn't want a bath at this time of day.'

'She'd better have one,' said Mary, quietly, out of submission.

Miss Louisa's gorge rose, and she was silent. When the little man padded down with the flannels on his arm, Mrs Lindley asked:

'Hadn't *you* better take a hot bath, Edward?'

But the sarcasm was lost on the little clergyman. He was absorbed in the preparations round the baby.

The room was dull and threadbare, and the snow outside seemed fairy-like by comparison, so white on the lawn and tufted on the bushes. Indoors the heavy pictures hung obscurely on the walls, everything was dingy with gloom.

Except in the fireglow, where they had laid the bath on the hearth. Mrs Massy, her black hair always smoothly coiled and queenly, knelt by the bath, wearing a rubber apron, and holding the kicking child. Her husband stood holding the towels and the flannels to warm. Louisa, too cross to share in the joy of the baby's bath, was laying the table. The boy was hanging on the door-knob, wrestling with it to get out. His father looked round.

'Come away from the door, Jack,' he said ineffectually. Jack tugged harder at the knob as if he did not hear. Mr Massy blinked at him.

'He must come away from that door, Mary,' he said. 'There will be a draught if it is opened.'

'Jack, come away from the door, dear,' said the mother, dextrously turning the shiny wet baby onto her towelled knee, then glancing around: 'Go and tell Aunt Louisa about the train.'

Louisa, also afraid to open the door, was watching the scene on the hearth. Mr Massy stood holding the baby's flannel, as if assisting at some ceremonial. If everybody had not been subduedly angry, it would have been ridiculous.

'I want to see out of the window,' Jack said. His father turned hastily.

'Do *you* mind lifting him onto a chair, Louisa?' said Mary hastily. The father was too delicate.

When the baby was flannelled, Mr Massy went upstairs and returned with four pillows, which he set in the fender to warm. Then he stood watching the mother feed her child, obsessed by the idea of his infant.

Louisa went on with her preparations for the meal. She could not have told why she was so sullenly angry. Mrs Lindley, as usual, sat silently watching.

Mary carried her child upstairs, followed by her husband with the pillows. After a while he came down again.

'What is Mary doing? Why doesn't she come down to eat?' asked Mr Lindley.

'She is staying with baby. The room is rather cold. I will ask the girl to put in a fire.' He was going absorbedly to the door.

'But Mary has had nothing to eat. It is *she* who will catch cold,' said the mother, exasperated.

Mr Massy seemed as if he did not hear. Yet he looked at his mother-in-law and answered:

'I will take her something.'

He went out. Mrs Lindley shifted on her couch with anger. Miss Louisa glowered. But no one said anything, because of the money that came to the vicarage from Mr Massy.

Louisa went upstairs. Her sister was sitting by the bed, reading a scrap of paper.

'Won't you come down and eat?' the younger asked.

'In a moment or two,' Mary replied in a quiet, reserved voice, that forbade anyone to approach her.

It was this that made Miss Louisa most furious. She went downstairs, and announced to her mother:

'I am going out. I may not be home to tea.'

CHAPTER EIGHT

No one remarked on her exit. She put on her fur hat, that the village people knew so well, and the old Norfolk jacket. Louisa was short and plump and plain. She had her mother's heavy jaw, her father's proud brow, and her own grey, brooding eyes that were very beautiful when she smiled. It was true, as the people said, that she looked sulky. Her chief attraction was the glistening, heavy deep-blonde hair, which shone and gleamed with a richness that was not entirely foreign to her.

'Where am I going?' she said to herself, when she got outside in the snow. She did not hesitate, however, but by mechanical walking found herself descending the hill towards Old Aldecross. In the valley that was black with trees, the colliery breathed in stertorous pants, sending out high conical columns of steam that remained upright, whiter than the snow on the hills, yet shadowy, in the dead air. Louisa would not acknowledge to herself whither she was making her way, till she came to the railway crossing. Then the bunches of snow in the twigs of the apple tree that leant towards the fence told her that she must go and see Mrs Durant. The tree was in Mrs Durant's garden.

Alfred was now at home again, living with his mother in the cottage below the road. From the highway hedge, by the railway crossing, the snowy garden sheered down steeply, like the side of a hole, then dropped straight in a wall. In this depth the house was snug, its chimney just level with the road. Miss Louisa descended the stone stairs, and stood below in the little backyard, in the dimness and the semi-secrecy. A big tree leant overhead, above the paraffin hut. Louisa felt secure from all the world down there. She knocked at the open door, then looked round. The tongue of garden narrowing in from the quarry bed was white with snow: she thought of the thick fringes of snowdrops it would show beneath the currant bushes in a month's time. The ragged fringe of pinks hanging over the garden brim behind her was whitened now with snowflakes, that in summer held white blossom to Louisa's face. It was pleasant, she thought, to gather flowers that stooped to one's face from above.

She knocked again. Peeping in, she saw the scarlet glow of the kitchen, red firelight falling on the brick floor and on the bright chintz cushions. It was alive and bright as a peepshow. She crossed the scullery, where still an almanac hung. There was no one about. 'Mrs Durant,' called Louisa softly, 'Mrs Durant.'

She went up the brick step into the front room, that still had its little shop counter and its bundle of goods, and she called from the stair-foot. Then she knew Mrs Durant was out.

She went into the yard, to follow the old woman's footsteps up the garden path.

She emerged from the bushes and raspberry canes. There was the whole quarry bed, a wide garden white and dimmed, brindled with dark bushes, lying half submerged. On the left, overhead, the little colliery train rumbled by. Right away at the back was a mass of trees.

Louisa followed the open path, looking from right to left, and then she gave a cry of concern. The old woman was sitting rocking slightly among the ragged, snowy cabbages. Louisa ran to her, found her whimpering with little, involuntary cries.

'Whatever have you done?' cried Louisa, kneeling in the snow.

'I've – I've – I was pulling a brussel-sprout stalk – and – oh-h! – something tore inside me. I've had a pain,' the old woman wept from shock and suffering, gasping between her whimpers – 'I've had a pain there – a long time – and now – oh, oh!' She panted, pressed her hand on her side, leant as if she would faint, looking yellow against the snow. Louisa supported her.

'Do you think you could walk now?' she asked.

'Yes,' gasped the old woman.

Louisa helped her to her feet.

'Get the cabbage – I want it for Alfred's dinner,' panted Mrs Durant. Louisa picked up the stalk of brussel-sprouts, and with difficulty got the old woman indoors. She gave her brandy, laid her on the couch, saying:

'I'm going to send for a doctor – wait just a minute.'

The young woman ran up the steps to the public house a few yards away. The landlady was astonished to see Miss Louisa.

'Will you send for a doctor at once to Mrs Durant,' she said, with some of her father in her commanding tone.

'Is something the matter?' fluttered the landlady in concern.

Louisa, glancing out up the road, saw the grocer's cart driving to Eastwood. She ran and stopped the man, and told him.

Mrs Durant lay on the sofa, her face turned away, when the young woman came back.

'Let me put you to bed,' Louisa said. Mrs Durant did not resist.

Louisa knew the ways of the working people. In the bottom drawer of the dresser she found dusters and flannels. With the old pit-flannel she snatched out the oven shelves, wrapped them up, and put them in the bed. From the son's bed she took a blanket, and, running down, set it before the fire. Having undressed the little old woman, Louisa carried her upstairs.

'You'll drop me, you'll drop me!' cried Mrs Durant.

Louisa did not answer, but bore her burden quickly. She could not light a fire, because there was no fireplace in the bedroom. And the floor was plaster. So she fetched the lamp, and stood it lit in one corner.

'It will air the room,' she said.

'Yes,' moaned the old woman.

Louisa ran with more hot flannels, replacing those from the oven shelves. Then she made a bran-bag, and laid it on the woman's side. There was a big lump on the side of the abdomen.

'I've felt it coming a long time,' moaned the old lady, when the pain was easier, 'but I've not said anything: I didn't want to upset our Alfred.'

Louisa did not see why 'our Alfred' should be spared.

'What time is it?' came the plaintive voice.

'A quarter to four.'

'Oh!' wailed the old lady, 'he'll be here in half an hour, and no dinner ready for him.'

'Let me do it?' said Louisa, gently.

'There's that cabbage – and you'll find the meat in the pantry – and there's an apple pie you can hot up. But *don't you* do it –!'

'Who will then?' asked Louisa.

'I don't know,' moaned the sick woman, unable to consider.

Louisa did it. The doctor came and gave serious examination. He looked very grave.

'What is it, doctor?' asked the old lady, looking up at him with old, pathetic eyes in which hope was already dead.

'I think you've torn the skin in which a tumour hangs,' he replied.

'Ay!' she murmured, and she turned away.

'You see, she may die any minute – and it *may* be swaled away,' said the old doctor to Louisa.

The young woman went upstairs again.

'He says the lump may be swaled away, and you may get quite well again,' she said.

'Ay!' murmured the old lady. It did not deceive her. Presently she asked:

'Is there a good fire?'

'I think so,' answered Louisa.

'He'll want a good fire,' the mother said. Louisa attended to it.

Since the death of Durant, the widow had come to church occasionally, and Louisa had been friendly to her. In the girl's heart the purpose was fixed. No man had affected her as Alfred Durant had done, and to that she kept. In her heart, she adhered to him. A natural sympathy existed between her and his rather hard, materialistic mother.

Alfred was the most lovable of the old woman's sons. He had grown up like the rest, however, headstrong and blind to everything but his own will. Like the other boys, he had insisted on going into the pit as soon as he left school, because that was the only way speedily to become a man, level with all the other men. This was a great chagrin to his mother, who would have liked to have this last of her sons a gentleman.

But still he remained constant to her. His feeling for her was deep and unexpressed. He noticed when she was tired, or when she had a new cap. And he bought little things for her occasionally. She was not wise enough to see how much he lived by her.

At the bottom he did not satisfy her, he did not seem manly enough. He liked to read books occasionally, and better still he liked to play the piccolo. It amused her to see his head nod over the instrument as he made an effort to get the right note. It made her fond of him, with tenderness, almost pity, but not with respect. She wanted a man to be fixed, going his own way without knowledge of women. Whereas she knew Alfred depended on her. He sang in the choir because he liked singing. In the summer he worked in the garden, attended to the fowls and pigs. He kept pigeons. He played on Saturday in the cricket or football team. But to her he did not seem the man, the independent man her other boys had been. He was her baby – and whilst she loved him for it, she was a little bit contemptuous of him.

There grew up a little hostility between them. Then he began to drink, as the others had done; but not in their blind, oblivious way. He was a little self-conscious over it. She saw this, and she pitied it in him. She loved him most, but she was not satisfied with him because he was not free of her. He could not quite go his own way.

Then at twenty he ran away and served his time in the Navy. This had made a man of him. He had hated it bitterly, the service, the subordination. For years he fought with himself under the military discipline, for his own self-respect, struggling through blind anger and shame and a cramping sense of inferiority. Out of humiliation and self-hatred he rose into a sort of inner freedom. And his love for his mother, whom he idealised, remained the fact of hope and of belief.

He came home again, nearly thirty years old, but naive and inexperienced as a boy, only with a silence about him that was new: a sort of dumb humility before life, a fear of living. He was almost quite chaste. A strong sensitiveness had kept him from women. Sexual talk was all very well among men, but somehow it had no application to living women. There were two things for him, the *idea* of women, with which he

41

sometimes debauched himself, and real women, before whom he felt a deep uneasiness, and a need to draw away. He shrank and defended himself from the approach of any woman. And then he felt ashamed. In his innermost soul he felt he was not a man, he was less than the normal man. In Genoa he went with an under-officer to a drinking house where the cheaper sort of girl came in to look for lovers. He sat there with his glass, the girls looked at him, but they never came to him. He knew that if they did come he could only pay for food and drink for them, because he felt a pity for them and was anxious lest they lacked good necessities. He could not have gone with one of them; he knew it, and was ashamed, looking with curious envy at the swaggering, easy-passionate Italian whose body went to a woman by instinctive impersonal attraction. They were men, he was not a man. He sat feeling short, feeling like a leper. And he went away imagining sexual scenes between himself and a woman, walking wrapt in this indulgence. But when the ready woman presented herself, the very fact that she was a palpable woman made it impossible for him to touch her. And this incapacity was like a core of rottenness in him.

So several times he went, drunk, with his companions, to the licensed prostitute houses abroad. But the sordid insignificance of the experience appalled him. It had not been anything really: it meant nothing. He felt as if he were not physically, but spiritually impotent: not actually impotent, but intrinsically so.

He came home with this secret, never-changing burden of his unknown, unbestowed self torturing him. His Navy training left him in perfect physical condition. He bathed and used dumb-bells, and kept himself fit. He played cricket and football. He read books and began to hold fixed ideas when he got home from the Fabians. He played his piccolo, and was considered an expert. But at the bottom of his soul was always this canker of shame and incompleteness, he was uneasy and felt despicable among all his confidence and superiority of ideas. He would have changed with any mere brute, just to be free of himself, to be free of this shame of self-consciousness. He saw some collier lurching straight forward without misgiving, pursuing his own satisfaction, and he envied him. Anything, he would have given anything for this spontaneity and this blind stupidity which went to its own satisfaction direct.

CHAPTER NINE

He was not unhappy in the pit. He was admired by the men, and well enough liked. It was only he himself who felt the difference between himself and the others. He seemed to hide his own stigma. But he was never sure that the others did not really despise him for a ninny, as being less a man than they were. Only he pretended to be more manly, and was surprised by the ease with which they were deceived. And, being naturally cheerful, he was happy at work. He was sure of himself there. Naked to the waist, hot and grimy with labour, they squatted on their heels for a few minutes and talked, seeing each other dimly by the light of the safety lamps, while the black coal rose jutting round them, and the props of wood stood like little pillars in the low, black, very dark temple. Then the pony came and the gang-lad with a message from Number 7, or with a bottle of water from the horse-trough or some news of the world above. The day passed pleasantly enough. There was an ease, a go-as-you-please about the day underground, a delightful camaraderie of men shut off alone from the rest of the world, in a dangerous place, and a variety of labour holing, loading, timbering, and a glamour of mystery and adventure in the atmosphere, that made the pit not unattractive to him when he had again got over his anguish of desire for the open air and the sea.

This day there was much to do and Durant was not in humour to talk. He went on working in silence through the afternoon.

'Loose-all' came, and they trampled to the bottom. The whitewashed underground office shone brightly. Men were putting out their lamps. They sat in dozens round the bottom of the shaft, down which black, heavy drops of water fell continuously into the sump. The electric lights shone away down the main underground road.

'Is it raining?' asked Durant.

'Snowing,' said an old man, and the younger was pleased. He liked to go up when it was snowing.

'It'll just come right for Christmas?' said the old man.

'Ay,' replied Durant.

'A green Christmas, a fat churchyard,' said the other sententiously.

Durant laughed, showing his small, rather pointed teeth.

The cage came down, a dozen men lined on. Durant noticed tufts of snow on the perforated, arched roof of the chain, and he was pleased. He wondered how it liked its excursion underground. But already it was getting soppy with black water.

He liked things about him. There was a little smile on his face. But underlying it was the curious consciousness he felt in himself.

The upper world came almost with a flash, because of the glimmer of snow. Hurrying along the bank, giving up his lamp at the office, he smiled to feel the open about him again, all glimmering round him with snow. The hills on either hand were pale blue in the dusk, and the hedges looked savage and dark. The snow was trampled between the railway lines. But far ahead, beyond the black figures of miners moving home, it became smooth again, spreading right up to the dark wall of the coppice.

To the west there was a pinkness, and a big star hovered half revealed. Below, the lights of the pit came out crisp and yellow among the darkness of the buildings, and the lights of Old Aldecross twinkled in rows down the bluish twilight.

Durant walked glad with life among the miners, who were

all talking animatedly because of the snow. He liked their company, he liked the white dusky world. It gave him a little thrill to stop at the garden gate and see the light of home down below, shining on the silent blue snow.

CHAPTER TEN

By the big gate of the railway, in the fence, was a little gate that he kept locked. As he unfastened it, he watched the kitchen light that shone onto the bushes and the snow outside. It was a candle burning till night set in, he thought to himself. He slid down the steep path to the level below. He liked making the first marks in the smooth snow. Then he came through the bushes to the house. The two women heard his heavy boots ring outside on the scraper, and his voice as he opened the door:

'How much worth of oil do you reckon to save by that candle, Mother?' He liked a good light from the lamp.

He had just put down his bottle and snap-bag and was hanging his coat behind the scullery door, when Miss Louisa came upon him. He was startled, but he smiled.

His eyes began to laugh – then his face went suddenly straight and he was afraid.

'Your mother's had an accident,' she said.

'How?' he exclaimed.

'In the garden,' she answered. He hesitated with his coat in his hands. Then he hung it up and turned to the kitchen.

'Is she in bed?' he asked.

'Yes,' said Miss Louisa, who found it hard to deceive him. He was silent. He went into the kitchen, sat down heavily in his father's old chair, and began to pull off his boots. He head was small, rather finely shapen. His brown hair, close and crisp, would look jolly whatever happened. He wore heavy, moleskin trousers that gave off the stale, exhausted scent of the pit. Having put on his slippers, he carried his boots into the scullery.

'What is it?' he asked, afraid.

'Something internal,' she replied.

He went upstairs. His mother kept himself calm for his coming. Louisa felt the tread shake the plaster floor of the bedroom above.

'What have you done?' he asked.

'It's nothing, my lad,' said the old woman, rather hard. 'It's nothing. You needn't fret, my boy, it's nothing more the matter with me than I had yesterday, or last week. The doctor said I've done nothing serious.'

'What were you doing?' asked her son.

'I was pulling up a cabbage, and I suppose I pulled too hard; for, oh – there was such a pain –'

He son looked at her quickly. She hardened herself.

'But who doesn't have a sudden pain sometimes, my boy? We all do.'

'And what's it done?'

'I don't know,' she said, 'but I don't suppose it's anything.'

The big lamp in the corner was screened with a dark green screen, so that he could scarcely see her face. He was strung tight with apprehension and many emotions. Then his brow knitted.

'What did you go pulling your inside out at cabbages for,' he asked, 'and the ground frozen? You'd go on dragging and dragging if you killed yourself.'

'Somebody's got to get them,' she said.

'You needn't do yourself harm.'

But they had reached futility.

Miss Louisa could hear plainly downstairs. Her heart sank. It seemed so hopeless between them.

'Are you sure it's nothing much, Mother?' he asked, appealing after a little silence.

'Ay, it's nothing,' said the old woman, rather bitter.

'I don't want you to – to – to be badly – you know.'

'Go an' get your dinner,' she said. She knew she was going to die: moreover, the pain was torture just then. 'They're only cosseting me up a bit because I'm an old woman. Miss Louisa's *very* good – and she'll have got your dinner ready, so you'd better go and eat it.'

He felt stupid and ashamed. His mother put him off. He had to turn away. The pain burned in her bowels. He went downstairs. The mother was glad he was gone, so that she could moan with pain.

He had resumed the old habit of eating before he washed himself. Miss Louisa served his dinner. It was strange and exciting to her. She was strung up tense, trying to understand him and his mother. She watched him as he sat. He was turned away from his food, looking in the fire. Her soul watched him, trying to see what he was. His black face and arms were uncouth, he was foreign. His face was masked black with coal-dust. She could not see him, she could only know him. The brown eyebrows, the steady eyes, the coarse, small moustache above the closed mouth – these were the only familiar indications. What was he, as he sat there in his pit dirt? She could not see him, and it hurt her.

She ran upstairs, presently coming down with the flannels and the bran-bag, to heat them, because the pain was on again.

He was halfway through his dinner. He put down the fork, suddenly nauseated.

'They will soothe the wrench,' she said. He watched, useless and left out.

'Is she bad?' he asked.

'I think she is,' she answered.

It was useless for him to stir or comment. Louisa was busy. She went upstairs. The poor old woman was in a white, cold sweat of pain. Louisa's face was sullen with suffering as she went about to relieve her. Then she sat and waited. The pain passed gradually, the old woman sank into a state of coma. Louisa still sat silent by the bed. She heard the sound of water downstairs. Then came the voice of the old mother, faint but unrelaxing –

'Alfred's washing himself – he'll want his back washing –'

Louisa listened anxiously, wondering what the sick woman wanted.

'He can't bear if his back isn't washed –' the old woman persisted, in a cruel attention to his needs. Louisa rose and wiped the sweat from the yellowish brow.

'I will go down,' she said soothingly.

'If you would,' murmured the sick woman.

Louisa waited a moment. Mrs Durant closed her eyes, having discharged her duty. The young woman went downstairs. Herself, or the man, what did they matter? Only the suffering woman must be considered.

Alfred was kneeling on the hearthrug, stripped to the waist, washing himself in a large panchion of earthenware. He did so every evening, when he had eaten his dinner; his brothers had done so before him. But Miss Louisa was strange in the house.

He was mechanically rubbing the white lather on his head, with a repeated, unconscious movement, his hand every now and then passing over his neck. Louisa watched. She had to brace herself to this also. He bent his head into the water, washing it free of soap, and pressed the water out of his eyes.

'Your mother said you would want your back washing,' she said.

Curious how it hurt her to take part in their fixed routine of life! Louisa felt the almost repulsive intimacy being forced upon her. It was all so common, so like herding. She lost her own distinctness.

He ducked his face round, looking up at her in what was a very comical way. She had to harden herself.

'How funny he looks with his face upside down,' she thought. After all, there was a difference between her and the common people. The water in which his arms were plunged was quite black, the soap-froth was darkish. She could scarcely conceive him as human. Mechanically, under the influence of habit, he groped in the black water, fished out soap and flannel, and handed them backwards to Louisa. Then he remained rigid and submissive, his two arms thrust straight in the panchion, supporting the weight of his shoulders. His skin was beautifully white and unblemished, of an opaque solid whiteness. Gradually Louisa saw it: this was also what he was. It fascinated her. Her feeling of separateness passed away: she ceased to draw back from contact with him and his mother. There was this living centre. Her heart ran hot. She had reached some goal in this beautiful clear male body. She loved him in a white impersonal heat. But the sunburnt, reddish neck and ears: they were more personal, more curious. A tenderness rose in her, she loved even his queer ears. A person – an intimate being he was to her. She put down the towel and went upstairs again, troubled in her heart. She had only seen one human being in her life – and that was Mary. All the rest were strangers. Now her soul was going to open, she was going to see another. She felt strange and pregnant.

'He'll be more comfortable,' murmured the sick woman abstractedly, as Louisa entered the room. The latter did not answer. Her own heart was heavy with its own responsibility. Mrs Durant lay silent awhile, then she murmured plaintively:

'You mustn't mind, Miss Louisa.'

'Why should I?' replied Louisa, deeply moved.

'It's what we're used to,' said the old woman.

And Louisa felt herself excluded again from their life. She sat in pain, with the tears of disappointment distilling in her heart. Was that all?

Alfred came upstairs. He was clean, and in his shirtsleeves. He looked a workman now. Louisa felt that she and he were foreigners, moving in different lives. It dulled her again. Or, if she could only find some fixed relations, something sure and abiding.

'How do you feel?' he said to his mother.

'It's a bit better,' she replied wearily, impersonally. This strange putting herself aside, this abstracting herself and answering him only what she thought good for him to hear, made the relations between mother and son poignant and cramping to Miss Louisa. It made the man so ineffectual, so nothing. Louisa groped as if she had lost him. The mother was real and positive – he was not very actual. It puzzled and chilled the young woman.

'I'd better fetch Mrs Harrison?' he said, waiting for his mother to decide.

'I suppose we shall have to have somebody,' she replied.

Miss Louisa stood by, afraid to interfere in their business. They did not include her in their lives, they felt she had nothing to do with them, except as a help from outside. She felt hurt and powerless against this unconscious difference. But something patient and unyielding in her made her say:

'I will stay and do the nursing: you can't be left.'

The other two were shy, and at a loss for an answer.

'We s'll manage to get somebody,' said the old woman wearily. She did not care very much what happened, now.

'I will stay until tomorrow in any case,' said Louisa. 'Then we shall see.'

'I'm sure you've no right to trouble yourself,' moaned the old woman. But she must leave herself in my hands.

Miss Louisa felt glad that she was admitted, even in an official capacity. She wanted to share their lives. At home they would need her now, now Mary had come. But they must manage without her.

'I must write a note to the vicarage,' she said.

Alfred Durant looked at her enquiringly, for her service. He had always that intelligent readiness to serve, since he had been in the Navy. But there was a simple independence in his willingness, which she loved. She felt nevertheless it was hard to get at him. He was so deferential, quick to take the slightest suggestion of an order from her, implicitly, that she could not get at the man in him.

He looked at her very keenly. She noticed his eyes were golden brown, with a very small pupil, the kind of eyes that can see a long way off. He stood alert, at military attention. His face was still rather weather-reddened.

'Do you want pen and paper?' he asked, with deferential suggestion to a superior, which was more difficult for her than reserve.

'Yes, please,' she said.

He turned and went downstairs. He seemed to her so self-contained, so utterly sure in his movement. How was she to approach him? For he would take not one step towards her. He would only put himself entirely and impersonally at her service, glad to serve her, but keeping himself quite removed from her. She could see he felt real joy in doing anything for her, but any recognition would confuse him and hurt him. Strange it was to her, to have a man going about the house in his shirtsleeves, his waistcoat unbuttoned, his throat bare, waiting on her. He moved well, as if he had plenty of life to spare. She was attracted by his completeness. And yet, when all was ready, and there was nothing more for him to do, she quivered, meeting his questioning look.

As she sat writing, he placed another candle near her. The rather dense light fell in two places on the overfoldings of her hair till it glistened heavy and bright, like a dense golden plumage folded up. Then the nape of her neck was very white, with fine down and pointed wisps of gold. He watched it as it were a vision, losing himself. She was all that was beyond him, of revelation and exquisiteness. All that was ideal and beyond him she was that – and he was lost to himself in looking at her. She had no connection with him. He did not approach her. She was there like a wonderful distance. But it was a treat, having her in the house. Even with this anguish for his mother tightening about him, he was sensible of the wonder of living this evening. The candle glistened on her hair, and seemed to fascinate him. He felt a little in awe of her, and a sense of uplifting, that he and she and his mother should be together for a time, the strange, unknown atmosphere. And, when he got out of the house, he was afraid. He saw the stars above ringing with fine brightness, with the snow beneath just visible, and a new night was gathering round him. He was afraid almost with obliteration. What was this new night ringing about him, and what was he? He could not recognise himself nor any of his surroundings. He was afraid to think of his mother. And yet his chest was conscious of her, and of what was happening to her. He could not escape from her, she carried him with her into an unformed, unknown chaos.

CHAPTER ELEVEN

He went up the road in an agony, not knowing what it was all about, but feeling as if a red-hot iron were gripped round his chest. Without thinking, he shook two or three tears onto the snow. Yet in his mind he did not believe his mother would die. He was in the grip of some greater consciousness. As he sat in the hall of the vicarage, waiting whilst Mary put things for Louisa into a bag, he wondered why he had been so upset. He felt abashed and humbled by the big house, he felt again as if he were one of the rank and file. When Miss Mary spoke to him, he almost saluted.

'An honest man,' thought Mary. And the patronage was applied as salve to her own sickness. She had station, so she could patronise: it was almost all that was left to her. But she could not have lived without having a certain position. She could never have trusted herself outside a definite place, nor respected herself except as a woman of superior class.

As Alfred came to the latch-gate, he felt the grief at his heart again, and saw the new heavens. He stood a moment looking northwards to the Plough climbing up the night, and at the far glimmer of snow in distant fields. Then his grief came on like physical pain. He held tight to the gate, biting his mouth, whispering, 'Mother!' It was a fierce, cutting, physical pain of grief, that came on in bouts, as his mother's pain came on in bouts, and was so acute he could scarcely keep erect. He did not know where it came from, the pain, nor why. It had nothing to do with his thoughts. Almost it had nothing to do with him. Only it gripped him and he must submit. The whole tide of his soul, gathering in its unknown towards the expansion into death, carried him with it helplessly, all the fritter of his thought consciousness caught up as nothing, the heave passing on towards its breaking, taking him further than he had ever been. When the young man had regained himself, he went indoors and there he was almost gay. It seemed to excite him. He felt in high spirits: he made whimsical fun of things. He sat on one side of his mother's bed, Louisa on the other, and a certain gaiety seized them all. But the nights and the dread was coming on.

Alfred kissed his mother and went to bed. When he was half undressed the knowledge of his mother came upon him, and the suffering seized him in its grip like two hands, in agony. He lay on the bed screwed up tight. It lasted so long, and exhausted him so much, that he fell asleep, without having the energy to get up and finish undressing. He awoke after midnight to find himself stone cold. He undressed and got into bed, and was soon asleep again.

At a quarter to six he woke, and instantly remembered. Having pulled on his trousers and lit a candle, he went into his mother's room. He put his hand before the candle flame so that no light fell on the bed.

'Mother!' he whispered.

'Yes,' was the reply.

There was a hesitation.

'Should I go to work?'

He waited, his heart was beating heavily.

'I think I'd go, my lad.'

His heart went down in a kind of despair.

'You want me to?'

He let his hand down from the candle flame. The light fell on the bed. There he saw Louisa looking up at him. Her eyes were upon him. She quickly shut her eyes and half buried her face in the pillow, her back turned to him. He saw the rough hair like bright vapour about her round head, and the two plaits flung coiled among the bedclothes. It gave him a shock. He stood almost himself, determined. Louisa cowered down. He looked, and met his mother's eyes. Then he gave way again, and ceased to be sure, ceased to be himself.

'Yes, go to work, my boy,' said the mother.

'All right,' replied he, kissing her. His heart was down at despair, and bitter. He went away.

'Alfred!' cried his mother faintly.

He came back with beating heart.

'What, Mother?'

'You'll always do what's right, Alfred?' the mother asked, beside herself in terror now he was leaving her. He was too terrified and bewildered to know what she meant.

'Yes,' he said.

She turned her cheek to him. He kissed her, then went away, in bitter despair. He went to work.

CHAPTER TWELVE

By midday his mother was dead. The word met him at the pit-mouth. As he had known, inwardly, it was not a shock to him, and yet he trembled. He went home quite calmly, feeling only heavy in his breathing.

Miss Louisa was still at the house. She had seen to everything possible. Very succinctly, she informed him of what he needed to know. But there was one point of anxiety for her.

'You *did* half expect it – it's not come as a blow to you?' she asked, looking up at him. Her eyes were dark and calm and searching. She too felt lost. He was so dark and inchoate.

'I suppose – yes,' he said stupidly. He looked aside, unable to endure her eyes on him.

'I could not bear to think you might not have guessed,' she said.

He did not answer.

He felt it a great strain to have her near him at this time. He wanted to be alone. As soon as the relatives began to arrive, Louisa departed and came no more. While everything was arranging, and a crowd was in the house, whilst he had business to settle, he went well enough, with only those uncontrollable paroxysms of grief. For the rest, he was super-ficial. By himself, he endured the fierce, almost insane bursts of grief which passed again and left him calm, almost clear, just wondering. He had not known before that everything could break down, and all be a great chaos, very vast and wonderful. It seemed as if life in him had burst its bounds, and was lost in a great, bewildering flood, immense and unpeopled. He himself was broken and spilled out amid it all. He could only breathe panting in silence. Then the anguish came on again.

When all the people had gone again from the Quarry

Cottage, leaving the young man alone, with an elderly housekeeper, then the long trial began. The snow had thawed and frozen, a fresh fall had whitened the grey, this then began to thaw. The world was a place of loose grey slosh. Alfred had nothing to do in the evenings. He was a man whose life had been filled up with small activities. Without knowing it, he had been centralised, polarised in his mother. It was she who had kept him. Even now, when the old housekeeper had left him, he might still have gone on in his old way. But the force and balance of his life was lacking. He sat pretending to read, all the time holding his fists clenched, and holding himself in, enduring he did not know what. He walked the black and sodden miles of field-paths, till he was tired out: but all this was only running away from whence he must return. At work he was all right. If it had been summer he might have escaped working in the garden till bedtime. But now, there was no escape, no relief, no help. He, perhaps, was made for action rather than for understanding; for doing than for being. He was shocked out of his activities, like a swimmer who forgets to swim.

For a week, he had the force to endure this suffocation and struggle, then he began to get exhausted, and knew it must come out. The instinct of self-preservation became strongest. But there was the question: Where was he to go? The public house really meant nothing to him, it was no good going there. He began to think of emigration. In another country he would be all right. He wrote to the emigration offices.

On the Sunday after the funeral, when all the Durant people had attended church, Alfred had seen Miss Louisa, impassive and reserved, sitting with Miss Mary, who was proud and very distant, and with the other Lindleys, who were people removed. Alfred saw them as people remote. He did not think

59

about it. They had nothing to do with his life. After service Louisa had come to him and shaken hands.

'My sister would like you to come to supper one evening if you would be so good.'

He looked at Miss Mary, who bowed. Out of kindness, Mary had proposed this to Louisa, disapproving of herself even as she did so. But she did not examine herself closely.

'Yes,' said Durant awkwardly, 'I'll come if you want me.' But he vaguely felt that it was misplaced.

'You'll come tomorrow evening, then, about half-past six.'

He went. Miss Louisa was very kind to him. There could be no music, because of the babies. He sat with his fists clenched on his thighs, very quiet and unmoved, lapsing, among all those people, into a kind of muse or daze. There was nothing between him and them. They knew it as well as he. But he remained very steady in himself, and the evening passed slowly. Mrs Lindley called him 'young man'.

'Will you sit here, young man?'

He sat there. One name was as good as another. What had they to do with him?

Mr Lindley kept a special tone for him, kind, indulgent, but patronising. Durant took it all without criticism or offence, just submitting. But he did not want to eat – that troubled him, to have to eat in their presence. He knew he was out of place. But it was his duty to stay yet awhile. He answered precisely, in monosyllables.

When he left he winced with confusion. He was glad it was finished. He got away as quickly as possible. And he wanted still more intensely to go right away, to Canada.

CHAPTER THIRTEEN

Two evenings after, Louisa tapped at the door of the Quarry Cottage, at half-past six. He had finished dinner, the woman had washed up and gone away, but still he sat in his pit dirt. He was going later to the New Inn. He had begun to go there because he must go somewhere. The mere contact with other men was necessary to him, the noise, the warmth, the forgetful flight of the hours. But still he did not move. He sat alone in the empty house till it began to grow on him like something unnatural.

He was in his pit dirt when he opened the door.

'I have been wanting to call – I thought I would,' she said, and she went to the sofa. He wondered why she wouldn't use his mother's round armchair. Yet something stirred in him, like anger, when the housekeeper placed herself in it.

'I ought to have been washed by now,' he said, glancing at the clock, which was adorned with butterflies and cherries, and the name of 'T. Brooks, Mansfield'. He laid his black hands along his mottled dirty arms. Louisa looked at him. There was the reserve, and the simple neutrality towards her, which she dreaded in him. It made it impossible for her to approach him.

'I am afraid,' she said, 'that I wasn't kind in asking you to supper.'

'I'm not used to it,' he said, smiling with his mouth, showing the interspaced white teeth. His eyes, however, were steady and unseeing.

'It's not *that*,' she said hastily. Her repose was exquisite and her dark grey eyes rich with understanding. He felt afraid of her as she sat there, as he began to grow conscious of her.

'How do you get on alone?' she asked.

He glanced away to the fire.

'Oh –' he answered, shifting uneasily, not finishing his answer.

Her face settled heavily.

'How close it is in this room. You have such immense fires. I will take off my coat,' she said.

He watched her take off her hat and coat. She wore a cream cashmere blouse embroidered with gold silk. It seemed to him a very fine garment, fitting her throat and wrists close. It gave him a feeling of pleasure and cleanness and relief from himself.

'What were you thinking about, that you didn't get washed?' she asked, half intimately. He laughed, turning aside his head. The whites of his eyes showed very distant in his black face.

'Oh,' he said, 'I couldn't tell you.'

There was a pause.

'Are you going to keep this house on?' she asked.

He stirred in his chair, under the question.

'I hardly know,' he said. 'I'm very likely going to Canada.'

Her spirit became very quiet and attentive.

'What for?'

Again he shifted restlessly on his seat.

'Well' – he said slowly – 'to try the life.'

'But which life?'

'There's various things – farming or lumbering or mining. I don't mind much what it is.'

'And is that what you want?'

He did not think in these times, so he could not answer.

'I don't know,' he said, 'till I've tried.'

She saw him drawing away from her for ever.

'Aren't you sorry to leave this house and garden?' she asked.

'I don't know,' he answered reluctantly. 'I suppose our Fred would come in – that's what he's wanting.'

'You don't want to settle down?' she asked.

He was leaning forward on the arms of his chair. He turned to her. Her face was pale and set. It looked heavy and impassive, her hair shone richer as she grew white. She was to him something steady and immovable and eternal presented to him. His heart was hot in anguish of suspense. Sharp twitches of fear and pain were in his limbs. He turned his whole body away from her. The silence was unendurable. He could not bear her to sit there any more. It made his heart go hot and stifled in his breast.

'Were you going out tonight?' she asked.

'Only to the New Inn,' he said.

Again there was silence.

She reached for her hat. Nothing else was suggested to her. She *had* to go. He sat waiting for her to be gone, for relief. And she knew that if she went out of that house as she was, she went out a failure. Yet she continued to pin on her hat; in a moment she would have to go. Something was carrying her.

Then suddenly a sharp pang, like lightning, seared her from head to foot, and she was beyond herself.

'Do you want me to go?' she asked, controlled, yet speaking out of a fiery anguish, as if the words were spoken from her without her intervention.

He went white under his dirt.

'Why?' he asked, turning to her in fear, compelled.

'Do you want me to go?' she repeated.

'Why?' he asked again.

'Because I wanted to stay with you,' she said, suffocated, with her lungs full of fire.

His face worked, he hung forward a little, suspended, staring straight into her eyes, in torment, in an agony of chaos,

63

unable to collect himself. And as if turned to stone, she looked back into his eyes. Their souls were exposed bare for a few moments. It was agony. They could not bear it. He dropped his head, whilst his body jerked with little sharp twitchings.

She turned away for her coat. Her soul had gone dead in her. Her hands trembled, but she could not feel any more. She drew on her coat. There was a cruel suspense in the room. The moment had come for her to go. He lifted his head. His eyes were like agate, expressionless, save for the black points of torture. They held her, she had no will, no life any more. She felt broken.

'Don't you want me?' she said helplessly.

A spasm of torture crossed his eyes, which held her fixed.

'I – I –' he began, but he could not speak. Something drew him from his chair to her. She stood motionless, spellbound, like a creature given up as prey. He put his hand tentatively, uncertainly on her arm. The expression of his face was strange and inhuman. She stood utterly motionless. Then clumsily he put his arms round her, and took her, cruelly, blindly, straining her till she nearly lost consciousness, till he himself had almost fallen.

Then, gradually, as he held her gripped, and his brain reeled round, and he felt himself falling, falling from himself, and whilst she, yielded up, swooned to a kind of death of herself, a moment of utter darkness came over him, and they began to wake up again as if from a long sleep. He was himself.

After a while his arms slackened, she loosened herself a little, and put her arms round him, as he held her. So they held each other close, and hid against each other for assurance, helpless in speech. And it was ever her hands that trembled more closely upon him, drawing him nearer into her, with love.

And at last she drew back her face and looked up at him, with eyes wet, and shining with light. His heart, which saw, was silent with fear. He was with her. She saw his face all sombre and inscrutable, and he seemed eternal to her. And all the echo of pain came back into the rarity of bliss, and all her tears came up.

'I love you,' she said, her lips drawn to sobbing. He put down his head against her, unable to hear her, unable to bear the sudden coming of the peace and passion that almost broke his heart. They stood together in silence whilst this thing moved away a little.

At last she wanted to see him. She looked up. His eyes were strange and glowing, with a tiny black pupil. Strange they were, and powerful over her. And his mouth came to hers, and slowly her eyelids closed, and his mouth sought hers closer and closer, and took possession of her.

They were silent for a long time, too much mixed up with passion and grief and death to do anything but hold each other in pain, and kiss with long, hurting kisses wherein fear was transfused into desire. At last she disengaged herself. He felt as it his heart were hurt, but glad, and he scarcely dared look at her.

'I'm glad,' she said also.

He held her hands in passionate gratitude and desire. He had not yet the presence of mind to say anything. He was dazed with relief.

'I ought to go,' she said.

He looked at her. He could not grasp the thought of her going, he knew he could never be separated from her any more. Yet he dared not assert himself. He held her hands tight.

'Your face is black,' she said.

He laughed.

'Yours is a bit smudged,' he said.

They were afraid of each other, afraid to talk. He could only keep her near to him. After a while she wanted to wash her face. He brought her some warm water, standing by and watching her. There was something he wanted to say, that he dared not. He watched her wiping her face, and making tidy her hair.

'They'll see your blouse is dirty,' he said.

She looked at her sleeves and laughed for joy.

He was sharp with pride.

'What shall you do?' he asked.

'How?' she said.

He was awkward at a reply.

'About me,' he said.

'What do you want me to do?' she laughed.

He put his hand out slowly to her. What did it matter!

'But make yourself clean,' she said.

CHAPTER FOURTEEN

As they went up the hill, the night seemed dense with the unknown. They kept close together, feeling as if the darkness were alive and full of knowledge, all around them. In silence they walked up the hill. At first the street lamps went their way. Several people passed them. He was more shy than she, and would have let her go had she loosened in the least. But she held firm.

Then they came into the true darkness, between the fields. They did not want to speak, feeling closer together in silence. So they arrived at the vicarage gate. They stood under the naked horse-chestnut tree.

'I wish you didn't have to go,' he said.

She laughed a quick little laugh.

'Come tomorrow,' she said, in a low tone, 'and ask Father.'

She felt his hand close on hers.

She gave the same sorrowful little laugh of sympathy. Then she kissed him, sending him home. At home, the old grief came on in another paroxysm, obliterating Louisa, obliterating even his mother, for whom the stress was raging like a burst of fever in a wound. But something was sound in his heart.

CHAPTER FIFTEEN

The next evening he dressed to go to the vicarage, feeling it was to be done, not imagining what it would be like. He would not take this seriously. He was sure of Louisa, and this marriage was like fate to him. It filled him also with a blessed feeling of fatality. He was not responsible, neither had her people anything really to do with it.

They ushered him into the little study, which was fireless. By and by the vicar came in. His voice was cold and hostile and he said:

'What can I do for you, young man?'

He knew already, without asking.

Durant looked up at him, again like a sailor before a superior. He had the subordinate manner. Yet his spirit was clear.

'I wanted, Mr Lindley –' he began respectfully, then all the colour suddenly left his face. It seemed now a violation to say what he had to say. What was he doing there? But he stood on, because it had to be done. He held firmly to his own independence and self-respect. He must not be indecisive. He must put himself aside: the matter was bigger than just his personal self. He must not feel. This was his highest duty.

'You wanted –' said the vicar.

Durant's mouth was dry, but he answered with steadiness:

'Miss Louisa – Louisa – promised to marry me –'

'You asked Miss Louisa if she would marry you – yes –' corrected the vicar. Durant reflected he had not asked her this:

'If she would marry me, sir. I hope you – don't mind.'

He smiled. He was a good-looking man, and the vicar could not help seeing it.

'And my daughter was willing to marry you?' said Mr Lindley.

'Yes,' said Durant seriously. It was pain to him, nevertheless. He felt the natural hostility between himself and the elder man.

'Will you come this way?' said the vicar. He led into the dining room, where were Mary, Louisa, and Mrs Lindley. Mr Massy sat in a corner with a lamp.

'This young man has come on your account, Louisa?' said Mr Lindley.

'Yes,' said Louisa, her eyes on Durant, who stood erect, in discipline. He dared not look at her, but he was aware of her.

'You don't want to marry a collier, you little fool,' cried Mrs Lindley harshly. She lay obese and helpless upon the couch, swathed in a loose dove-grey gown.

'Oh hush, Mother,' cried Mary, with quiet intensity and pride.

'What means have you to support a wife?' demanded the vicar's wife roughly.

'I!' Durant replied, starting. 'I think I can earn enough.'

'Well, and how much?' came the rough voice.

'Seven and six a day,' replied the young man.

'And will it get to be any more?'

'I hope so.'

'And are you going to live in that poky little house?'

'I think so,' said Durant, 'if it's all right.'

He took small offence, only was upset, because they would not think him good enough. He knew that, in their sense, he was not.

'Then she's a fool, I tell you, if she marries you,' cried the mother roughly, casting her decision.

'After all, Mama, it is Louisa's affair,' said Mary distinctly, 'and we must remember –'

'As she makes her bed, she must lie – but she'll repent it,' interrupted Mrs Lindley.

'And after all,' said Mr Lindley, 'Louisa cannot quite hold herself free to act entirely without consideration for her family.'

'What do you want, Papa?' asked Louisa sharply.

'I mean that if you marry this man, it will make my position very difficult for me, particularly if you stay in this parish. If you were moving quite away, it would be simpler. But living here in a collier's cottage, under my nose, as it were – it would be almost unseemly. I have my position to maintain, and a position which may not be taken lightly.'

'Come over here, young man,' cried the mother, in her rough voice, 'and let us look at you.'

Durant, flushing, went over and stood – not quite at attention, so that he did not know what to do with his hands. Miss Louisa was angry to see him standing there, obedient and acquiescent. He ought to show himself a man.

'Can't you take her away and live out of sight?' said the mother. 'You'd both of you be better off.'

'Yes, we can go away,' he said.

'Do you want to?' asked Miss Mary clearly.

He faced round. Mary looked very stately and impressive. He flushed.

'I do if it's going to be a trouble to anybody,' he said.

'For yourself, you would rather stay?' said Mary.

'It's my home,' he said, 'and that's the house I was born in.'

'Then' – Mary turned clearly to her parents – 'I really don't see how you can make the conditions, Papa. He has his own rights, and if Louisa wants to marry him –'

'Louisa! Louisa!' cried the father impatiently. 'I cannot understand why Louisa should not behave in the normal way. I cannot see why she should only think of herself, and leave her family out of count. The thing is enough in itself, and she ought to try to ameliorate it as much as possible. And if –'

'But I love the man, Papa,' said Louisa.

'And I hope you love your parents, and I hope you want to spare them as much of the – the loss of prestige as possible.'

'We *can* go away to live,' said Louisa, her face breaking to tears. At last she was really hurt.

'Oh, yes, easily,' Durant replied hastily, pale, distressed.

There was dead silence in the room.

'I think it would really be better,' murmured the vicar, mollified.

'Very likely it would,' said the rough-voiced invalid.

'Though I think we ought to apologise for asking such a thing,' said Mary haughtily.

'No,' said Durant. 'It will be best all round.' He was glad there was no more bother.

'And shall we put up the banns here or go to the registrar?' he asked clearly, like a challenge.

'We will go to the registrar,' replied Louisa decidedly.

Again there was a dead silence in the room.

'Well, if you will have your own way, you must go your own way,' said the mother emphatically.

All this time Mr Massy had sat obscure and unnoticed in a corner of the room. At this juncture he got up, saying:

'There is baby, Mary.'

Mary rose and went out of the room, stately; her little husband padded after her. Durant watched the fragile, small man go, wondering.

'And where,' asked the vicar, almost genial, 'do you think you will go when you are married?'

Durant started.

'I was thinking of emigrating,' he said.

'To Canada? Or where?'

'I think to Canada.'

'Yes, that would be very good.'

Again there was a pause.

'We shan't see much of you then, as a son-in-law,' said the mother, roughly but amicably.

'Not much,' he said.

Then he took his leave. Louisa went with him to the gate. She stood before him in distress.

'You won't mind them, will you?' she said humbly.

'I don't mind them, if they don't mind me!' he said. Then he stooped and kissed her.

'Let us be married soon,' she murmured, in tears.

'All right,' he said. 'I'll go tomorrow to Barford.'

BIOGRAPHICAL NOTE

David Herbert Lawrence was born in Nottinghamshire in 1885. The child of a miner, Lawrence was brought up in poverty and ill health. His mother encouraged him to go to school, which he did until the age of fifteen, when he was forced to take a job as a clerk in a factory. Determined to be educated, he saved up the twenty-pound fee, and won a scholarship to Nottingham University College.

Lawrence's first novel, *The White Peacock*, appeared in 1911. During this time he also wrote poetry and short stories. After his mother died, Lawrence became very ill, and the experiences of these years went on to form the basis of *Sons and Lovers* (1913). In 1912, his life changed when he met and fell in love with Frieda, the wife of his university professor. They eloped to Germany and lived a nomadic life, while Lawrence wrote travel books. During the First World War, the couple moved back to England and Lawrence produced *The Rainbow* (1916), which was impounded for its sexual explicitness. *Women in Love*, which he finished in 1917, faced similar problems, but eventually found a New York publisher in 1920. After the war, Lawrence and his wife began to travel again, to Australia, Italy and Mexico. His most famous novel, *Lady Chatterley's Lover*, was written while he was dying of tuberculosis. Published in a private edition by a friend of Lawrence's in 1928, it caused such a scandal that New York and London editions didn't appear until thirty years later. Lawrence, meanwhile, had died in Vence in the south of France in 1930.

SELECTED TITLES FROM HESPERUS PRESS